Darkness

by
Anne Schraff

Perfection Learning® Corporation

Logan, Iowa 51546

Editor: Pegi Bevins
Cover Illustration: Doug Knutson
Cover Design: Deborah Lea Bell
Michael A. Aspengren

For information, contact
Perfection Learning® Corporation
1000 North Second Avenue, P.O. Box 500
Logan, Iowa 51546-0500.
Tel: 1-800-831-4190 • Fax: 1-712-644-2392
Paperback ISBN 0-7891-5183-9
Cover Craft® ISBN 0-7807-9367-6
Printed in the U.S.A.

1 Seventeen-year-old Karl Schmidt hurried into Mr. Wagner's room. He slid into his seat right before the bell rang. Karl breathed a sigh of relief. American history was definitely the one class he didn't want to be late for. Albert Wagner was a hard-nosed young man who ran his class like a drill sergeant. He did not tolerate tardiness and accepted no excuses.

Karl glanced behind him to see if Rebecca Silverman had arrived. His stomach fluttered a little when he saw her. Today she had on a pink sweater that set off her dark, curly hair and large brown eyes. And when she turned her head, Karl could see the graceful curve of her neck and shoulders in profile. Karl thought Rebecca was beautiful in an exotic way.

Rebecca had come to Westphalia High School at the beginning of winter semester in January. Karl had developed a crush on her immediately. But for the last few weeks, he'd been too shy to approach such a pretty girl. He had spoken to her a few times. But only when they worked on group projects together in class. Finally, over the weekend, he'd made up his mind to ask Rebecca out. But the whole week had gone by, and Karl still had not worked up the nerve to approach her. Now it was Friday. And on the way to school that morning, Karl had promised himself that today was the day. He would wait for Rebecca after class and ask her to go to the drugstore after school for a root beer float. It was not like a real date, but it was a start.

But as he gazed Rebecca's way, he noticed that she looked troubled. Her brow was wrinkled. And she stared at the desk in front of her as if she were in deep thought. Karl wondered if it had anything to do with the latest news. Yesterday, March 15, 1939, Germany had invaded Czechoslovakia.

As Karl looked around the classroom, he noticed that most of the kids were talking excitedly about the events of that week. Karl could hear the words "Hitler" and "war" in some of the conversations. Stephen Franks and David Hummel seemed to be most excited of all. The two blond-haired, blue-eyed boys who could have passed for brothers laughed and slapped one another on the back. "Go, Germany!" Karl heard Stephen say.

Just then Mr. Wagner called the class to order. He had a crisp, staccato voice that sliced through the air. "*Achtung!*" he said, using German as he sometimes did.

Westphalia, Ohio, was a predominantly German town. It had been settled by German immigrants in the 1850s. They had named it after Westphalia, Germany, where most of the immigrants were from. Even though they spoke English, many of the citizens still sprinkled their speech with German words. So everyone in class knew that *achtung* meant "attention."

For the last two weeks, the class had been doing a unit on the Civil War. But Mr. Wagner always started out each period with a discussion of current events.

"Who knows what happened in Czechoslovakia yesterday?" Mr. Wagner asked.

David Hummel immediately raised his hand. "The Czechs were taken over by the Germans," he said with obvious enthusiasm.

"That's right," Mr. Wagner answered. "I'm glad to see you're keeping up on current events, David."

David smiled proudly.

Karl frowned. Mr. Wagner was engaged to David's older sister. It seemed like the teacher always treated David special.

"And why did Germany invade Czechoslovakia?" Mr. Wagner probed. Stephen Franks raised his hand. "Stephen?"

"Hitler said it was because the Germans living there were being mistreated by the Czechs," he said.

"Exactly," the teacher said, smiling in approval. "Germany's boundaries were changed after the Great War of 1914. As a result, an area with about three million Germans became part of Czechoslovakia. Hitler is simply protecting his own people."

His smile faded slightly when Rebecca's hand went up. "Rebecca?" he said.

"I heard that those Germans were not being mistreated at all," she said. "That Hitler just used that as an excuse to take over Czechoslovakia."

"And where did you hear that?" Mr. Wagner asked doubtfully.

Rebecca hesitated. Then she said, "From my uncle."

Karl heard David and Stephen snicker. "From her *Jew* uncle!" one of them whispered.

"That figures," the other whispered back.

"Come now, Rebecca," Mr. Wagner replied. "Do you mean to tell me that your uncle knows more than the news media? It's all over the newspapers and radios what happened. Are you saying news journalists lie?"

Rebecca lowered her eyes. "I didn't mean to say they lied," she said quietly. "I just think there's a lot of misinformation around."

"Well, certainly, there's always misinformation surrounding an event of this magnitude," Mr. Wagner conceded. "But the German government was just doing what was right—protecting its own. Let's turn the tables for a moment, Rebecca. If Americans were being mistreated in, say, Mexico, don't you think the United States government would have a right—and a duty—to protect its people?"

"Well, yes . . ." Rebecca began, "but—"

"Fine, then we agree," Mr. Wagner said.

Heidi Zimmerman raised her hand. "Heidi?" Mr. Wagner said.

"Do you think Germany will stop with Czechoslovakia?" Heidi asked. "Last year it took over Austria. So this is the second European country it's invaded."

"Austria was originally part of Germany," Mr. Wagner explained. "Hitler was simply taking back what rightfully belonged to the German people." Then he smiled and added, "In answer to your question, Heidi, yes, Hitler will stop now. He has promised that he will seek no new territory."

"But what about Poland?" another student asked. "I heard talk that he already has his eye on Poland."

"Yeah, I think Poland's next," David said. He ran his finger across his throat and said, "Kerrrch!"

Stephen and a few other students laughed.

"Adolf Hitler is an honorable man. I'm sure he will keep his promise," Mr. Wagner said.

Rebecca raised her hand again. "I don't think Hitler will stop with Czechoslovakia," she said with worry in her voice. "I think he plans on taking over all of Eastern Europe."

Mr. Wagner looked annoyed now. "Rebecca, that is simply not factual. The two countries have a treaty. Neither will show aggression toward the other for at least 10 years. You are giving a highly charged opinion."

"But—" Rebecca began.

"Hitler has made a promise," Mr. Wagner said, cutting her off again. "We can be sure he will keep it."

As always, Karl was impressed with Rebecca's knowledge of what was going on in Europe. Rebecca was Jewish and had come to the United States from Germany. Karl didn't know why, but she lived with her aunt and uncle in Westphalia. But he had heard her tell a friend that her parents still lived in Germany and often wrote letters about what was happening there.

Karl wasn't sure what to think about Germany. He knew that Adolf Hitler was an odd-looking little man who had a Charlie Chaplin mustache and seemed to talk in a constant scream. And he had heard that Hitler was wildly popular among the German people. But it worried Karl that no one had lifted a finger to stop the Germans when they marched into Austria the year before. Now Hitler had taken over Czechoslovakia. Would he really stop there? Karl wondered.

As the end of the period approached, Karl grew more and more nervous. Every time he looked at Rebecca's face, he lost more of his confidence. She was so pretty. Why would she want to spend time with someone as nondescript as he was? Karl was tall and lanky with almost colorless blond hair and pale blue eyes. He considered himself bland compared to Rebecca's striking features.

Karl sighed. Oh, well, I guess all she can do is turn me down, he told himself. And who knows, maybe she'll accept. He made up his mind to approach Rebecca after class.

At the end of the period, Mr. Wagner said, "Don't forget, class. Test on Monday."

Some of the students groaned, Karl among them. Guess I know what I'll be doing this weekend, he thought.

When the bell rang, Karl scooped up his books and hurried out to catch Rebecca. She was only a few feet down the hall when he reached the door. "Rebecca!" he called.

Rebecca turned around and smiled. "Hello, Karl," she replied.

"Say, you were really impressive in class today," Karl said, catching up to her. "You know so much about what's going on in the world."

Rebecca smiled again, but this time it was a sad smile. "Unfortunately, I know too much," she said.

"Wish I had that problem," Karl said, chuckling. "I don't seem to know enough. Just ask Mr. Wagner. He'll tell you."

"Mr. Wagner doesn't know everything," Rebecca said quietly.

"Maybe not, but he's in charge of the grade book, and that's what counts," Karl said. Then he remembered why he had stopped her. He took a deep breath and felt his mouth go dry. Finally he said, "Um, Rebecca, I was just wondering—and feel free to say no—I'll understand. But do you think you might like to go to the drugstore with me after school and get a root beer float?"

Karl was pleased to see the sadness leave Rebecca's face and her eyes light up. "I'd like that very much, Karl," she said.

"You would? I mean, swell," Karl said. "I'll meet you at the front doors after school."

"See you then, Karl," Rebecca called as she turned down the next hallway toward her second period class.

"Yeah, see you," Karl said. He felt a rush of happiness as he headed toward his locker. He'd done it! He'd actually asked her out—and she had said yes! He counted his money for the second time that day. He had just enough to buy them each a root beer float if he skipped lunch. He'd be hungry in his afternoon classes, he knew, but Rebecca was worth it!

* * *

After school, Karl and Rebecca crossed the street in a stream of Westphalia High students. Some were going to the drugstore for ice cream or a soda. Others were heading toward the bus stop or toward home. Very few students had cars, even among the seniors. The Depression had hit hard in Westphalia. It was a struggle for most people just to keep a family car running. Almost no one could afford a second car for a son or daughter.

Karl and Rebecca found two stools at the counter in the drugstore. Karl ordered two super-deluxe root beer floats with double scoops of ice cream. He wanted to impress Rebecca.

They waited in silence for their order. Karl was still nervous and wasn't sure what to say. He cleared his throat more times than was necessary and pivoted back and forth on his stool. Finally he blurted out, "It's better to get two scoops of ice cream. With only one scoop, you run out and have only root beer left."

"Hmm," Rebecca said, nodding her head.

Oh, brother, that was a clever thing to say, Karl thought. I'm really impressing her now.

Just then their order came. Two large fountain glasses with double scoops of vanilla ice cream floating in pools of creamy brown liquid. "Looks good, huh?" Karl asked.

"Oh, yes," Rebecca replied, smiling. She took the straw between her red lips and sipped delicately.

Again Karl noticed how pretty she looked. He decided to try to strike up a conversation again.

"That was really great how you spoke up in history about Europe," he said. "You're really smart."

Rebecca's smile faded, and worry lines returned to her brow. "Mr. Wagner didn't like what I had to say. I guess Hitler is very popular, even in this country."

"Why is he so popular?" Karl wanted to know.

Rebecca took another sip of her float and then asked, "Do you know anything about the Great War of 1914, Karl?"

Karl shrugged. "A little," he said. "I

know it was Germany's fault."

"Well, that's not entirely true," Rebecca replied. "But Germany was blamed for it. When the war ended, Germany lost everything—its colonies, much of its land. And it was deeply in debt to France and England. The German people were humiliated. They had a weak military and a weak government. Millions of them lost their jobs, causing them to live in poverty. Ever since the war, the Germans have been looking for a strong leader. One who could improve things in Germany. Hitler's doing that—at least for some people. He's creating jobs and giving the Germans hope."

Again Karl was impressed with Rebecca's knowledge. "Wow! How do you know all that?" he asked.

Rebecca smiled. "My Uncle Jacob was a history professor at a university in Germany. I live with him and Aunt Helga here in Westphalia. He and I have long talks about what's going on in Europe."

"Why did your uncle come to the United States?" Karl asked. "It sounds like he had a good job in Germany."

"He did," Rebecca said. "He was one of the most respected professors at the university in Berlin. He wrote books and traveled all over Europe giving lectures. Then the Nazis came into power—"

"The Nazis?" Karl asked.

"The National Socialists—Hitler's political party. The Nazis passed a law that said that only non-Jews could work for the government. That included teachers in public schools and universities. One day Uncle Jacob went to work and found he had been replaced. That was when he decided it was time to leave the country. He and Aunt Helga have been here for about five years."

"But that's terrible!" Karl exclaimed. "How can Hitler get away with that?"

Rebecca shrugged and replied sadly, "Because no one is stopping him."

Karl thought about that a minute. Could a leader really do things like that in the 20th century? he wondered. And why would the German people allow it? For that matter, why would the Jews allow it?

"Can I ask you something else, Rebecca?" he asked.

"Yes, Karl," Rebecca said, taking another sip of her float.

"Why did you come to the United States? And why didn't your parents come with you?"

Rebecca sighed and stirred her float. Then she spoke in a voice barely above a whisper. "*Kristallnacht.*"

Karl frowned. "What?"

"Last November the Nazis organized a violent movement against the Jews," Rebecca said. "One night they began burning our synagogues—over a thousand of them. They trashed and looted thousands of Jewish businesses. They destroyed our cemeteries, our schools, our homes. Even some of our hospitals. Dozens of Jewish people were killed." She paused for a moment and took a deep, shaky breath. Then she pushed her glass away as if she had lost her appetite. "That night became known as *Kristallnacht*—the 'Night of Broken Glass'—for the shattered glass from store windows that littered the streets."

Karl couldn't believe what he was hearing. He had heard that Hitler did not like Jews. But this was the first time he'd been told that the Jews were actually being mistreated.

"After that night, all Jewish children were expelled from public schools," Rebecca went on. "My parents—"

"Wait a minute," Karl said, interrupting. "You were *expelled* from public schools?"

"Oh, yes," Rebecca answered. "We had already been forbidden to go to public playgrounds and swimming pools. And to museums and libraries. Anyway, my parents sent me here to America so I would be safe and could continue my education."

"But why didn't they come with you?" Karl asked. He couldn't imagine why any Jew would remain in Germany after what Rebecca had just told him.

"My father is a doctor," Rebecca explained. "He did not want to abandon the people who needed him. Jews are only allowed to be treated by Jewish doctors. My mother serves as his nurse. And together they see patients at one of the few remaining Jewish hospitals in Berlin, where we are from."

"Are they coming to the United States someday?" Karl wanted to know.

"Yes, they plan on coming soon, maybe even this spring," Rebecca said. "But it is not easy for Jews to obtain the necessary papers to leave Germany. And it's very expensive."

For a long time, Karl was silent. Like Rebecca, he had lost his appetite. His glass sat half full on the counter in front of him. Finally he spoke. "Surely someone will stop Hitler," he said. "No one can get away with doing things like that forever."

"I'm afraid he might be unstoppable, Karl," Rebecca said, shaking her head. "Now he has all the people from Austria and Czechoslovakia under his power. His army will grow and grow. I think what my Uncle Jacob said last night makes sense."

"What did your uncle say?" Karl asked.

Rebecca sighed sadly and said, "That, if left unchecked, Hitler won't stop until he has conquered the world."

2 When Karl got home that afternoon, he found his mother at the kitchen table reading a letter. His eight-year-old sister, Katrina, was sitting beside her cutting out clothes for paper dolls.

Karl's ancestors on both sides of his family had been among the original immigrants who settled Westphalia. But some of his relatives still lived in Germany. Today his mother had received a letter from her cousin, Berta, who lived with her husband and son in Berlin.

"Oh, Karl, I'm so glad you're home," Mrs. Schmidt said. "Look what my cousin Berta enclosed in her letter. A picture of Josef. I can't believe how he has grown. He's 10 already! Doesn't he look handsome in his uniform? Berta says the shirt is brown and the shorts are black."

She handed Karl a black and white photograph of her second cousin. Karl set his books down on the table and looked at the picture.

"He looks like you, Karl," Katrina said.

Katrina was right. Like Karl, Josef was tall and slender. He had blond hair and light-colored eyes, probably blue like Karl's.

"Cousin Berta writes that Josef is doing very well," Karl's mother continued. "He's in some kind of youth organization called *Jungvolk.*"

"What's that mean, Mama?" Katrina asked.

"It's German for 'young folk,' Katie," Mrs. Schmidt replied. "It must be like the Boy Scouts. Berta says that if he does well, he could eventually become an officer in the German army. Isn't that wonderful?"

"Yeah, that's great, Mom," Karl said, looking at the photograph more closely. Josef was dressed in a shirt, shorts, and knee socks with heavy, black marching boots. On the left sleeve of the shirt Karl could see a distorted, black cross-like object. Its ends were bent at right angles. Karl vaguely remembered having seen one before, but he wasn't sure what it was. But what struck Karl most was what he saw in Josef's eyes. A kind of gleam he'd never seen in anyone's eyes before. An arrogant, superior gleam as if Josef were better than the viewer of the photograph. As if Josef were better than *anyone*.

"What's that thing on his sleeve?" Katrina asked.

"It's a swastika," her mother replied, gazing at the picture Karl held. "The symbol of the new government in Germany. I suppose you could say it's like the bald eagle in the United States." She returned her attention to the letter.

I am so proud of my little Josef, Mrs. Schmidt read on. *He has all the makings of a fine German citizen. His father, however, disapproves of Josef's participation in the youth group. But you know Emil. He's such a fault-finder. He even disapproves of our new leader, Adolf Hitler. Can you imagine? Hitler is doing so much for Germany. There are many more jobs. We're eating well. Oh, you should be here, Johanna. There's a unified feeling among the people. I can't explain it. But finally after all these years, we Germans have something to hope for. Herr Hitler promises that he will win back our lost lands and make Germany a great nation again.*

Mrs. Schmidt wiped her eyes with the corner of her apron. "I'm so happy for them," she said. "Berta and Emil—and all the German people—have suffered for so long. They deserve a new leader—one who can do great things for Germany."

"Is Hitler a good leader, Mama?" Katrina asked.

"It sounds like he's very good," Mrs. Schmidt answered.

Karl handed the photograph of Josef back to his mother. "Mom, I was talking to a girl from Germany. She just came here a few months ago," he said.

"Oh? Who is that?" his mother asked, getting up to start supper. She laid the letter and photograph on the corner of the counter.

"Rebecca Silverman," Karl replied. "She said things are getting bad for the Jews in Germany."

Mrs. Schmidt frowned as she removed a pot from a cabinet. "I've never heard that," she said, setting the pot in the sink and filling it with water. "What part of Germany is she from?"

"Berlin," Karl answered. "She says the

Nazis destroyed Jewish synagogues and hospitals there," Karl said. "And that they won't let Jewish children attend public schools."

Karl's mother set the pot on the stove and added a heaping tablespoon of salt to the water. Then she took out several potatoes from under the sink. "But surely Berta would have mentioned that in her letter," his mother said as she peeled a potato. "The German citizens would never allow something like that to happen."

"That's what Rebecca says," Karl replied. "Her uncle lost his job in Germany because he's Jewish. He lives here in Westphalia now."

"Well, her uncle may have lost his job. But I doubt that it had anything to do with his being Jewish," Mrs. Schmidt said. She stopped working for a minute and looked at her son. "Karl, when something bad happens to people, like getting fired from a job, they often look for someone or something to blame. Your friend's uncle probably lost his job because he was incompetent. Not because he's Jewish."

She wiped her hands on a towel and

began dropping the potatoes into the pot of water. "No," she said, shaking her head, "if things like that were happening in Germany, Berta would have said so in her letter. Perhaps your friend just has an overactive imagination. Pick up your books now, dear, and start setting the table. We'll be eating soon. Katrina, take your paper dolls into the other room."

Karl set his books on the counter. As he removed four plates from the cabinet, he thought about what his mother had said. Could Rebecca have been exaggerating about what had happened in Germany? He had certainly never heard of *Kristallnacht*. Of course, he didn't pay much attention to the news. But wouldn't he have heard *something* about it? And maybe Rebecca's Uncle Jacob *was* looking for someone to blame for his misfortune. Rebecca had said that her uncle was one of the most respected professors at the university. Why would the Germans replace someone with so much to offer? That would be like cutting off your nose to spite your face.

* * *

Karl got to history class early on Monday morning. He wanted to spend a few minutes reviewing for the Civil War test. He had studied most of Sunday afternoon but still didn't feel confident about the names and dates of the major battles.

Several other students, including Rebecca Silverman, had the same idea. As Karl sat down, Rebecca looked up and smiled. Then she quickly returned her attention to her textbook.

Karl was encouraged. At least she hadn't ignored him. He opened his book and started studying.

Mr. Wagner walked in a few minutes later and took attendance. When the bell rang, he asked the class to put their books away. Karl closed his book and placed it atop the notebook on his desk. As he picked up the stack to put it under his chair, something fluttered to the floor. Karl bent down to pick it up and saw that it was the picture of Berta's son Josef. It must have gotten mixed up with his school things over the weekend.

"What have we here?" Mr. Wagner asked as he placed a test on Karl's desk. He glanced at the picture Karl held in his hands. "A photograph? Is that you, Karl?" the teacher asked, noticing the light-colored hair and eyes.

"No, it's a cousin from Germany," Karl answered.

"May I?" Mr. Wagner asked.

Karl handed him the picture. "Ah, yes, a *Jungvolk*," Mr. Wagner said approvingly. "I've heard quite a bit about these remarkable children."

He held up the picture for the class to see. Karl heard a small gasp come from behind him. He glanced back and saw Rebecca staring wide-eyed at the picture.

Mr. Wagner handed the photo back to Karl and continued around the room with the test. "*Jungvolk*, for those of you who don't know, is the junior branch of the Hitler Youth organization."

"What's that?" one student asked.

"The Hitler Youth organization is made up of children who are devoted to the German cause," Mr. Wagner said. "These children undergo rigorous training to become the best German citizens they can possibly be."

"Sounds like fun," Stephen Franks said.

"It's not fun, I can assure you," Mr. Wagner said. "It requires devotion and diligence. However, from what I have read, these youth are destined to become great leaders. They will probably one day be surrounded by glory. What young person wouldn't want that?"

He handed out the last test and returned to his desk at the front of the room. "Thank you for bringing your cousin's photograph, Karl. You must be very proud of him."

"But I—" began Karl.

Mr. Wagner cut him off. "Now, to work, *Klasse!*" he said. "No more talking."

Karl glanced at Rebecca again. The worry had returned to her brow. Why would the picture of Josef bother her? he wondered.

With an effort, he turned his attention to his test. It didn't look too hard after all. The short-answer section would be tricky. He knew Mr. Wagner was a stickler for using exact wording in short answers. But the true and false questions looked fairly easy. And he was glad that most of the questions about the battles were in the multiple choice section. At least the answers were there. He just had to make the right choices. Even the essay question was manageable. "Name a major author from the Civil War era and explain why his or her writings were important. Your essay should be at least one page long." Karl had read a lot about Frederick Douglass, the ex-slave who became an abolitionist. He could easily write a page on Douglass.

Karl worked hard for the rest of the period and handed in his test just before the bell rang. As he left the classroom, he saw Rebecca waiting for him.

"Hi," Karl said as he approached. "How'd you do?"

Rebecca ignored his question. "Karl, I have to talk to you."

"What's up?" Karl asked.

"Was that really your cousin in the photograph Mr. Wagner had?" she asked. Karl noticed the concern in her voice.

"My mom's second cousin," Karl replied.

"Josef. He's 10 years old."

"Karl, do you know what members of the Hitler Youth do?" Rebecca asked.

Karl shrugged. "My mom said they're like Boy Scouts. Mr. Wagner said they're being trained to be leaders. That's all I know."

"Karl, the Hitler Youth are nothing like Boy Scouts," Rebecca insisted. "They roam the cities in gangs, burning crosses on lawns and beating up on people."

Karl frowned and asked, "Who do they do that to?"

"Anyone who's not like them—Jews, Gypsies, or anyone of color. They call them 'Undesirables,' " Rebecca replied. "Once I saw them attack an old Jewish man in the street. They started out by taunting him. They took away his cane and pulled his beard. They pushed him back and forth between them. Then they started shoving him hard. He fell to the ground, and one boy kicked him. The others joined in. Then one picked up the old man's cane and began beating him about the head with it. They didn't stop until the old man was unconscious. Then they threw the cane down and walked away laughing."

"Why didn't someone stop them?" Karl asked.

"There was a German policeman standing nearby," Rebecca said. "He simply watched and did nothing."

Karl was appalled at Rebecca's story. But at the same time, he wondered if she was really telling the truth. Had she imagined this incident to be worse than it was?

"Rebecca, are you sure?" Karl asked. "Maybe they didn't really hurt the man all that much."

Rebecca looked into Karl's eyes and said, "Karl, I saw the cane in the street the next day. The end of it was covered with blood."

Karl shook his head. "But how can that be?" he asked. "I can't imagine Berta and her husband allowing Josef to do such things."

Rebecca laughed a short, harsh laugh that surprised Karl. "They have no say in what Josef does now," she said.

"What do you mean?" Karl asked.

"From now on, your cousin belongs to the Nazis," Rebecca said. "His parents have been replaced—by Hitler himself!"

Just then Stephen and David approached. "Hey, Karl," David said. "Let's see that picture of your cousin again."

"Hey, guys, I didn't bring it to show it around," Karl explained. "It just got mixed in with my homework."

"Come on, let's see it," David demanded, holding out his hand and clicking his fingers impatiently.

Reluctantly, Karl dug the picture out of his notebook and handed it to David.

"Wow, that is *some* uniform," David said. He nudged Stephen in the ribs. "I bet if we wore something like that to school, the girls would all go for us, huh?"

Stephen laughed and punched David in the arm. "You know what they say about a man in uniform," he said.

Karl looked at Rebecca. She was standing silently, staring at the floor. He could see that she felt uneasy around the two boys.

"Look, I've got to get to class," Karl said. "Can I have it back now?"

"Here," David said, handing the photo back. "Hey, write to your cousin and see if he'll send us each one of those uniforms," he added jokingly.

"Yeah, great idea," Stephen agreed. "Then we can be *Jungvolk* and work for Hitler." He raised his arm in salute and snapped his heels together. Then he looked straight at Rebecca and said in a German accent, "*Heil* Hitler!"

The two boys laughed as they walked away.

When the boys had gone, Karl asked, "What's the matter, Rebecca? Don't you like those two?"

Rebecca shook her head. "They scare me," she said. "They're too much like the boys I went to school with in Berlin."

"They're harmless," Karl said.

Rebecca looked into Karl's eyes and said, "If there's one thing I've learned in the last few months, Karl, it's that *no one* is harmless."

3 A few days later, Mr. Wagner handed back the tests over the Civil War. Karl was pleased. He'd gotten a *B*, which was pretty good for him. He glanced back at Rebecca. She was frowning at her test.

"Any questions about the test?" Mr. Wagner asked.

Rebecca raised her hand. "I have a question about the first one in the short answer section."

"What is it?" Mr. Wagner said. Karl thought he could detect impatience in the teacher's voice.

"I put 'the War Between the States' for the answer, and you counted it wrong," Rebecca said.

"That's because it *is* wrong," Mr. Wagner replied. He read the question aloud. " 'What is the name of the struggle that occurred in the United States between 1861 and 1865?' The correct answer is 'the Civil War.' I've warned all of you before to use exact wording in your answers. Next question?"

But Rebecca wasn't finished. "Excuse me, Mr. Wagner," she said politely, "but isn't the War Between the States the same thing as the Civil War?" she asked.

Mr. Wagner sighed. "The *official* name of the struggle, Rebecca, is the *Civil War*," he said.

"But—" Rebecca began.

"Next question!" Mr. Wagner said with finality in his voice.

Karl glanced around the room. Across from him, Stephen Franks was showing his test to David Hummel. Stephen pointed to a question, and they both snickered quietly. Leaning over, Karl could see that Stephen had the same answer Rebecca had. But Stephen had gotten credit for it. There was no red check mark next to what he wrote.

Karl glanced at Rebecca. She was leafing through her test, looking puzzled.

Two students asked questions, and then Rebecca raised her hand again. This time Mr. Wagner sighed audibly before calling on her. "*Yes*, Rebecca. What is it *now?*"

"For the essay question, I wrote about Frederick Douglass. I explained who he was and how his writings helped the cause of antislavery. I wrote almost two pages. You only gave me five points out of twenty-five, Mr. Wagner. Is that right?"

Mr. Wagner's eyes blazed. "Are you questioning my judgment, Rebecca?" he snapped. "Who is the teacher here, and who is the student? Frederick Douglass was a black man, which means he was a *minor* writer during the time period. I asked you to choose a *major* writer of the time period. You'd have been better off writing about Mark Twain or Emily Dickinson."

Karl checked his essay question. He had written just over a page about Frederick Douglass and had gotten 20 points out of 25! He raised his hand.

"Yes, Karl," Mr. Wagner barked.

"Excuse me, sir," Karl began, "but I wrote about Frederick Douglass, and you gave me 20 out of 25."

Mr. Wagner glared at Karl. "Very well," he seethed. "Rebecca, submit your test at the end of the period. I will review it."

Karl heard Stephen whisper to David, "He should have kept his mouth shut. Doesn't he know he's helping out a *Jew*-girl?"

"Yeah, Schmidt," Stephen said, reaching over and tapping Karl on the shoulder. "What's the matter with you?"

Karl looked at the two boys. He had known them both since grade school. He'd never been best friends with them, but the three had always gotten along. But now for the first time he was seeing a look in their eyes he'd never seen before. And it surprised him. Because it was the same look he'd seen in Josef's eyes.

* * *

The Depression put many men in Westphalia out of work. But Karl's father was a government employee. He worked at the local post office. So his was one of the few secure jobs in town. Because of this, the Schmidts were able to afford a telephone, something most families did without.

That night Karl called Rebecca. She sounded down.

"What's the matter?" Karl asked.

"I don't know," Rebecca replied. "Nothing, I guess."

"Come on, Rebecca, something's wrong. Tell me," Karl said.

"Karl, have you ever noticed the way

Mr. Wagner treats me?" Rebecca asked.

Karl frowned and said, "What do you mean?"

"He doesn't like me," Rebecca repeated. "You saw what happened with my test today."

"That was just a mistake," Karl said. "Anyone can make mistakes."

"No, it's more than that," Rebecca replied. "He's always treated me—differently. I think it's because I'm Jewish."

"Rebecca, that's ridiculous," Karl said. "Why would Wagner care if you're Jewish?"

Rebecca shrugged. "He's German."

"Well, so am *I*," Karl said. "And *I* don't care if you're Jewish."

"I know you don't, Karl," Rebecca said. "And most people in Westphalia don't care either. But some do. People like Mr. Wagner—and Stephen and David."

"Rebecca, I think you're being paranoid," Karl said. "There are many Jewish families in town. I've never heard of any discrimination here."

"Karl, there's discrimination against

Jews everywhere," Rebecca countered. "It's always been that way. Don't you see?"

"What do you mean?" Karl asked.

"Throughout history, people have had the misconception that all Jews are rich and that they control all the money," Rebecca explained. "So if people are poor, they naturally blame it on the Jews."

"But there *are* a lot of wealthy Jewish people in the world, aren't there?" Karl asked, remembering what he'd heard over the years.

"There are some, of course," Rebecca said. "But many more are poor. Jews are not all rich bankers and jewelers. The Jews I knew in Germany were farmers, tailors, accountants, factory workers. *None* of them was rich. And yet they're being blamed for Germany's financial problems. Did you know that the Jews were even blamed for causing the Black Plague during the Middle Ages?"

"I thought the plague was caused by fleas carried by rats," Karl said.

"It *was*," Rebecca replied. "But people didn't know that back then. So they blamed the Jews. Jews have been the world's scapegoats for centuries. So why does it surprise you that there might be discrimination here in Westphalia? My own aunt and uncle have been victims."

"They have?" Karl asked in surprise. "What happened?"

Rebecca was silent for a moment. Then she said, "I don't suppose you know what the Nuremberg Laws are, do you, Karl?"

"I don't think so," Karl replied.

"Remember when I told you that my father could only treat Jews?" Rebecca asked. "Well, that was because of the Nuremberg Laws."

"Okay. So what does that have to do with your aunt and uncle?" Karl wanted to know.

"The Nuremberg Laws affected Jews in many ways," Rebecca began. "All Jews lost their voting rights. Jewish business owners were forced to sell their business to Germans—usually at very low prices. Jewish lawyers were not allowed to practice law. And Jews were not allowed to marry Germans. If a Jew and a German were already married, the marriage was considered invalid. Basically, the

Nuremberg Laws made Jews second-class citizens."

"I still don't understand what that has to do with your aunt and uncle," Karl pressed.

"Uncle Jacob is Jewish. And Aunt Helga is German," Rebecca said. "They were married before the Nuremberg Laws were passed. In fact, they had already left Germany by then. But someone here in Westphalia must have heard about the Nuremberg Laws. They wrote my aunt a letter telling her she is living in sin with a filthy Jew—a 'Jew-pig' they called Uncle Jacob. They said that the marriage was no longer legal and that she should move out of the house before something happens to both of them. They signed the letter 'The Anonymous Aryan.' "

"Who in Westphalia would do such a thing?" Karl demanded.

"I don't know," Rebecca said. "But now do you believe me? There *are* people in Westphalia who don't like Jews—and I think Mr. Wagner is one of them."

4 For the next couple of weeks Karl watched the newspapers and listened to the radio for news about Germany. He wanted to ascertain whether Rebecca's stories about Germany were true. Or whether, as his mother had said, Rebecca simply had an overactive imagination.

But news from Germany was sparse. Other than an occasional mention of Hitler's name and the Nazi party, Karl heard very little news—either good or bad—about Germany.

"What's this sudden interest in Hitler and Germany, Karl?" his father asked one evening as they sat in front of the radio.

"I have a friend at school who says that the Nazis are persecuting the Jews in Germany," Karl explained. "I just wanted to find out if it's true. What do you think, Dad?"

"Well, I don't know about that, son," Mr. Schmidt said, picking up his pipe and filling it with tobacco. "I've heard that many Jews are leaving Germany, but that doesn't mean they're being persecuted. But I'll tell you one thing—that Hitler bothers me. He's too much of a fanatic for my tastes. Anybody who's *that* extreme about anything is dangerous. I just hope the German people realize it before it's too late."

"What do you mean?" Karl asked.

Karl waited while his father lit his pipe. Soon the familiar smell of cherry tobacco drifted over to Karl's nose.

"The Germans are looking for a quick fix to their problems—unemployment, poverty, low morale," his father explained. "And I can't blame them. They've suffered a lot since the Great War. But when people are that desperate, it's pretty easy for one determined person to lead them where *he* wants them to go. Hitler's promising them the moon, and they believe him. The only thing is, he's becoming a full-blown dictator in the meantime. And I don't think they realize it."

"But everyone says he's just what Germany needs," Karl remarked. "Even Berta and Mom say it."

"There's never been a good dictator, Karl, not in all of history," Mr. Schmidt replied. "It might look like Hitler is good for Germany right now. From what Berta says, he's creating jobs and putting food on people's plates. That would look good to anybody."

He stopped speaking to take a puff on his pipe. "But it's the long run the German people should be looking at. Dictators usually start out by taking away the rights of a few—the minority. Most people hardly notice. But sooner or later, they take away the rights of the majority too. And by that time, the dictator has total control, and no one can do anything about it."

* * *

When Karl entered Mr. Wagner's room the next day, Rebecca was waiting for him. Her eyes sparkled with excitement.

"Karl, I have wonderful news!" she said, following him to his desk.

"What's that, Rebecca?" Karl asked. As always, he was thrilled to see her. Since that first date at the drugstore, he and Rebecca had gone out several times. Karl felt at ease with Rebecca now and no longer had a hard time making conversation. The two enjoyed each other's company and seemed to have fun, no matter what they did.

"I got a letter from my parents yesterday. They're leaving Germany next month!"

Rebecca said. "They're taking an ocean liner from Hamburg—the *S.S. St. Louis*. Just think, Karl—they'll be here by summer! Isn't that wonderful?"

"That's great, Rebecca," Karl said. "But what about your father's work?"

Rebecca's voice saddened. "The Nazis have taken away Father's medical license. He is no longer allowed to practice medicine. He's now working as an orderly in a hospital for non-Jews." She shook her head and added, "My father, a brilliant doctor, is giving people sponge baths and emptying bedpans."

"Gosh, that's a shame," Karl sympathized. "But at least they're getting out of Germany. What day are they leaving?"

"May 13," Rebecca replied, her face brightening. "They've managed to get visas permitting them to enter Cuba. And they're on a waiting list to get into the United States."

"Waiting list? What do you mean?" Karl asked.

Rebecca laughed and said, "Karl, don't you keep up with anything? The United States lets in only so many immigrants per year. My parents will have to wait in Cuba until the U.S. allows them to enter. It shouldn't be more than a few weeks, though."

"I really am glad for you, Rebecca," Karl said. But then a disturbing thought hit him. What if Rebecca's parents came and moved her away from Westphalia? He might never see her again. "Do they plan on settling here in Westphalia?" he asked.

"They didn't say," Rebecca replied. "I'm sure if father can find work, we'll stay. After all, we have relatives here. But I can't say for . . . " Her voice trailed off as she realized what Karl was implying. "I hadn't thought of that, Karl," she said. "I wouldn't want to move away. I like it here—with you."

Suddenly Karl heard kissing sounds. He turned and saw Stephen and David mocking Rebecca.

"Hey, knock it off, you two," Karl said. "And quit listening to other people's conversations."

"Make us," David challenged.

"Yeah," Stephen chimed in. "Why are you wasting your time on her, Schmidt?"

"As if we have to ask," David said. "We

all know about Jew girls . . ."

"What are you implying?" Karl demanded.

David started to say something, but just then Mr. Wagner walked into the room.

Karl glared at David and Stephen, who were snickering by now. "Don't let those two get to you," he whispered to Rebecca.

Rebecca smiled a small smile. "I'll try," she said. Then she turned and went to her desk.

Karl sat down and opened his history book to chapter six. Since the Civil War unit, they had moved on to the Industrial Revolution.

"Klasse, let's continue our discussion on the Industrial Revolution in the United States," Mr. Wagner said. "Who can tell me the approximate years it occurred?"

Both Rebecca and Heidi raised their hands.

"Heidi?" Mr. Wagner said.

"1850–1900," Heidi replied.

"Good, good," the teacher said. "Now who can name one development that made the Industrial Revolution possible?"

Again Rebecca raised her hand, as did

Karl and several other students. Mr. Wagner called on Karl.

"The expansion of the railroads across the U.S. made the transportation of goods possible," he said.

"Yes," Mr. Wagner said, nodding his head. "Something else that made the revolution possible?"

Rebecca raised her hand for a third time, but Mr. Wagner called on Stephen.

"Machines were developed to mass-produce products," Stephen offered.

"*Gut,*" Mr. Wagner praised, falling back on his German. "Something else?"

This time only Rebecca raised her hand at first. Mr. Wagner looked past her, as if not seeing her. His eyes scanned the classroom. After a few seconds, David raised his hand. "David?" Mr. Wagner said.

"The flow of immigrants into the United States," David said.

Karl looked at Rebecca. Slowly she lowered her hand.

"Exactly," the teacher said. He glanced down at the book he held in his hands "According to your text, between 1848 and 1860, over 4,000,000 immigrants came into this country. And—this might interest most of you—1,000,000 of them were Germans. Nearly 25 percent. That's when many of our ancestors came and settled right here in Westphalia."

Heidi raised her hand. "How many immigrants are coming into the country today?" she asked.

"Not nearly as many," Mr. Wagner replied. "The Immigration Act of 1924 reduced the number of immigrants to 164,000. And it only allows a limited number of people from certain areas of the world."

"Why?" another student asked.

"The United States wants to restrict the number of undesirables entering the country," Mr. Wagner explained. "Too many foreigners from, say, Southern and Eastern Europe would upset the racial balance of the country."

"What do you mean—racial balance?" Stephen asked.

"Many of the people from those countries have dark features—the Italians, the Hungarians, and the Jews, for instance," Mr. Wagner said. "Americans want to keep their society pure."

Then he looked directly at Rebecca and said, "And, *for the most part*, they have. Look around you. The majority of you are fair-haired with light-colored eyes and skin—good German stock."

Karl glanced around the room. Mr. Wagner was right. Like Karl, the rest of the students looked very "German." Their hair color ranged from light blond to medium brown. And almost everyone had blue, gray, or green eyes.

Then his eyes fell on Rebecca. She was the one dark-featured student in the room. He looked around again. Everyone else was staring at her too. Rebecca lowered her eyes. Her cheeks colored to a deep rose-pink. She sat perfectly still, looking straight down at her desk as if she were ashamed to meet the other students' gazes. Karl felt sorry for Rebecca being singled out like that. He wished she would look up so he could catch her eye. He wanted to smile at her and make her feel better. But her gaze never left her desk.

"The United States is just like Germany then," Stephen said smugly, throwing a meaningful glare Rebecca's way. "I heard that Hitler wants to create a master race of Aryans."

"What's an Aryan?" Heidi asked.

"Aryans are—well, just a minute," Mr. Wagner said. "I'll show you." He went to his desk and took out a tape measure. "My aunt is a teacher in Germany. She wrote me about a little experiment they do there. Heidi, come up here, please," he said.

As Mr. Wagner spoke, Karl saw Rebecca snap to attention for a brief second. When she looked up, he was startled to see panic in her eyes. But before he could catch her attention, she lowered her gaze again.

Heidi was a pretty girl with large, blue eyes and ashen blond braids that hung down her back. Obediently, she walked to the front of the room. Meanwhile, Mr. Wagner had gone to the chalkboard and written "Heidi" in large letters. Then he walked over to Heidi and placed the end of the tape measure just above the bridge of her nose. Heidi and many of the students giggled.

"Now, hold still. This won't take but a minute," Mr. Wagner said. He brought the tape measure over the top of Heidi's head and down to the base of her skull. Then he turned and wrote the measurement on the board.

"Now, turn sideways, Heidi," the teacher said. Heidi complied.

Mr. Wagner held the tape measure against Heidi's nose. Again the class giggled. The teacher wrote this new measurement on the board. Next to it he added the word "straight." Then he wrote "Hair color: blond. Eye color: blue."

"Thank you, Heidi. You may sit down," Mr. Wagner said without turning around. He then wrote "Rebecca" next to Heidi's name. "Now, Rebecca, come to the front of the room," he said.

Rebecca slowly raised her eyes. "I . . . I'd rather not," she mumbled.

"Come now, Rebecca," Mr. Wagner said. "This doesn't hurt. And it will only take a minute."

Rebecca said nothing. For part of a second, her eyes met Karl's. Then she dropped her gaze to the desk again.

"Rebecca, to the front—now!" Mr. Wagner barked.

Slowly Rebecca rose to her feet. She moved away from her desk with effort, as if she were held there by a magnet. When she reached the front of the room, the teacher took her by the shoulders and turned her around to face the class.

By now Rebecca's face was burning with embarrassment. Either Mr. Wagner didn't notice or he didn't care. He measured her head and then her nose. He wrote the measurements on the chalkboard, adding the word "hooked" next to the nose length. Then he wrote "Hair color: black. Eye color: dark brown."

"Sit down, Rebecca," he said curtly.

Without meeting anyone's eyes, Rebecca returned to her seat. There she resumed staring at her desk.

"All right, what do you notice about the two girls' measurements?" Mr. Wagner asked.

Immediately David raised his hand. "Heidi's head is bigger," he said.

"That's right," the teacher replied. "Aryans have larger heads than non-Aryans. Which proves what?"

"Aryans are smarter," Stephen said.

"Exactly," Mr. Wagner said, nodding his head. "Smarter *and* more creative. Even more coordinated. In other words, the brain function of an Aryan is superior to that of a non-Aryan."

"And Rebecca's nose is longer. And it's hooked!" another student said. Several students laughed.

Karl glanced at Rebecca. He noticed that she had covered her nose with her hand.

"That's right," the teacher replied. "An unattractive feature, wouldn't you agree? Also, Aryans, like Heidi, have blond hair and blue eyes. Non-Aryans have darker, less desirable features. So you can clearly see that Heidi here is a member of the superior Aryan race. While Rebecca is a member of the inferior non-Aryan race." He glanced smugly around the room. "Any questions?"

No hands went up, but Karl noticed that many of the students were now looking at Rebecca with disdain.

"All right, *Klasse*, you have the rest of the period to finish reading chapter 7," Mr. Wagner said. "*Stille!*"

Karl opened his book and tried to read. But he had a hard time concentrating. He was bothered by what had just happened.

Why would Mr. Wagner embarrass Rebecca like that? he wondered. First he had refused to call on her. Then he had made her take part in a humiliating "experiment." Karl was beginning to think that Rebecca was right. Mr. Wagner *was* prejudiced against her.

After class, Karl hurried to catch up with Rebecca. But she moved quickly down the hall, as if she wanted nothing to do with anyone.

"Rebecca, wait!" he called. He ran up and placed his hand on her shoulder. "I'm sorry about what just happened," he said. "That stuff about brain function is a bunch of baloney. You know that."

When Rebecca turned around, Karl saw tears streaming down her face. "I know that," she said, "but you saw the others— they believe it!"

Karl sighed and shook his head. "I can't believe Wagner did that. I know how you must feel."

"Know how I feel?" she demanded. "How can you know how I feel?"

"Well, I—" Karl began, but Rebecca cut him off.

"Do you know how it feels to be treated

as an inferior, Karl?" she asked. "Do you know how it feels to have people look at you and doubt that you are capable of anything noble or grand? To have them think that you are less than human and that your place is in the sewer with the rats and cockroaches? Do you know what it feels like to be blamed for everything that goes wrong? Do you know those things, Karl? Have you experienced them?"

"Well, no, but—" Karl said.

"Have you heard what the Nazis call us?" Rebecca interrupted again. " 'A race of murderers and criminals who live off other races.' How can you *possibly* know how that feels?"

Karl began again. "I'm sorry, Rebecca. I didn't mean to . . ." His voice faded off as he struggled for the right thing to say.

Rebecca wiped at her tears with the back of her hand. She took a deep breath in an effort to gain control. "One day in Germany a teacher did the same "experiment" on me that Mr. Wagner just did," she said. "I was humiliated. But it was even worse this time. In Germany, Hitler is telling the Germans to hate us. Here in America, no one is telling them that—they are hating us on their own!"

Karl didn't know what to say. Rebecca was right. He had no idea how she felt. Karl had never experienced anything close to what she had just gone through. He had always had plenty of friends, had always fit in. His father had a good job, and his family was respected in the community. Karl could never even remember being truly humiliated in his life. What could he possibly know about discrimination?

"You're right, Rebecca," he said, taking her hand in his. "I *don't* know what you just went through. But I want you to know that I don't feel like some of the others do. I like you for who you are. Not because you're Jewish or because you're not Jewish. But just because you're *you*—Rebecca Silverman. Now, can you understand how *I* feel?"

Rebecca sniffed and dried the last of her tears. The faintest hint of a smile appeared on her lips. "No," she said. "But I'm glad you feel that way."

5 As scheduled, on Saturday, May 13, the *S.S. St. Louis* left Germany and sailed toward Cuba. Rebecca called Karl the next day to tell him. "My uncle phoned the shipping line in Hamburg," she said. "They told him that the ship left at 8:00 last night. And that my parents were aboard. Oh, Karl, I'm so excited. I can hardly wait to see my mother and father again!"

"That's wonderful, Rebecca," Karl said.

"Karl, we're having a special dinner tonight—to celebrate my parents' leaving Germany," Rebecca said. "Aunt Helga told me I could invite you. Would you like to come?"

"Sure I would," Karl said.

"Wonderful. Come over about 6:00," Rebecca said.

"I'll be there," said Karl.

That evening, Karl approached the neat brick house with the arched doorway. He had been to Jacob and Helga Silverman's house several times to pick up Rebecca for their dates. But he had always waited politely in the entryway. Now Rebecca escorted him into the living area of the house.

"Karl!" Uncle Jacob said as the two entered a large room with gleaming hardwood floors and overstuffed furniture. He took off his spectacles and put down the book he was reading. Then he rose from his rocking chair and shook Karl's hand warmly. "Thank you for joining our joyous celebration," he said.

"Thank you for inviting me, sir," Karl said.

Uncle Jacob was small man with a beard that reached almost to his waist. Like Rebecca, he had dark, curly hair and brown eyes.

Karl heard a tinkle of ice cubes and turned to see Helga Silverman entering the room. She was carrying four glasses of lemonade on a tray. In contrast to her husband, Aunt Helga had fair hair and green eyes.

"Welcome," she said, smiling at Karl. "Please sit down."

"Thank you," Karl said, sitting next to Rebecca on a green and gold flowered sofa. He glanced around. The room was colorful and warm. Delicate lace curtains framed the windows, and multicolored tapestry rugs covered sections of the floor. Paintings of landscapes and seascapes hung on the walls. A stone fireplace graced one end of the room. Above it hung a skillfully etched mirror.

A huge bookcase covered the greater portion of one wall. Karl could see volumes of historical books and remembered that Jacob Silverman had been a history professor. On the spines of other books, Karl recognized the names of famous people—Albert Einstein, Helen Keller, Ernest Hemingway.

In one corner stood a polished grand piano. On it Karl could see open sheet music as if someone had played recently.

"Lemonade, Karl?" Aunt Helga asked.

"Please," Karl said, accepting a glass. He nodded at the piano. "Do you play?" he asked.

"A little," Aunt Helga answered, smiling.

"Don't be so modest, Aunt Helga," Rebecca chided. Then she turned to Karl. "Aunt Helga was a concert pianist in Germany. Now she's teaching me how to play. And she's a wonderful teacher."

Aunt Helga blushed. "Thank you, dear," she said, smiling.

"So, Rebecca has told you the good news, eh?" Uncle Jacob asked as his wife handed him a frosty glass.

"Yes, she has," Karl replied, taking a sip of the cool, tart liquid.

"Within a few weeks, my younger brother and his wife will arrive," Uncle Jacob beamed. "Oh, how long I have waited for them to come to America. For years I have been writing them. 'Come!' I kept saying. 'Leave Germany. Make a new life for yourself here in America.' But they were reluctant to leave Berlin. And who can blame them? It is such a beautiful city, you know—the museums, the parks, the universities. And the libraries—probably the most beautiful of all."

He glanced at the book he had been reading. "Do you read, Karl?" he asked, picking up the book. Karl read the cover. *The Call of the Wild* by Jack London. He had heard of Jack London but had never read anything by him.

"Not much," Karl admitted.

"One should read," Uncle Jacob said

sagaciously. "It expands the mind. Here's a book I think you would like." He tapped the cover of the novel he held. "I brought this with me from Germany."

"You brought *all* your books with you, Uncle Jacob," Rebecca laughed, indicating the huge bookcase.

"As many as I could," Uncle Jacob admitted, standing up and walking over to the bookcase. He ran his hand lovingly over the covers of the books and shook his head sadly. "Do you know that many of these books are no longer allowed in Germany, Karl?" he said.

"What do you mean?" Karl asked.

"The Nazis destroyed them in the book burnings of 1933," Uncle Jacob replied.

Karl frowned. "Book burnings?" he asked.

"Right before Helga and I left—let's see, that would have been in May of 1933. The Nazis raided libraries and bookstores across Germany," he explained. "They marched by torchlight in nighttime parades. They sang chants and threw the books into huge bonfires. More than 25,000 books were burned in one night."

"What books did they burn?" Karl wanted to know. "And why?"

"Some of the books were by Jewish writers—Sigmund Freud, Albert Einstein. Here is one of Einstein's works," he said, pointing to a huge, leather-bound volume. "They burned those books simply because they were written by Jews. But most of the books were by non-Jewish writers— Ernest Hemingway, Sinclair Lewis, Helen Keller. Any author who spoke for freedom and dignity of the human spirit. The Nazis know that it's easier to rule people once the people get it out of their heads that they should rule themselves. Even this book, *The Call of the Wild*, was burned. Can you imagine, Karl? A book in which the main character is a dog!"

Karl shook his head. He was getting more confused every day. Here was another Nazi horror story that he hadn't heard about.

"Mr. Silverman, can you tell me what's going on in Germany?" he asked. "I listen to the news and read the newspapers, but I don't see anything about book burnings or laws that take away people's rights. My

mom's cousin lives in Berlin. She says
things haven't been this good in Germany
since before the Great War."

"No doubt things *are* good for her,"
Uncle Jacob commented. "That's because
she is probably what the Nazis consider a
'pure German.' The Nuremberg Laws
define 'Jew' as anyone having three or
four Jewish grandparents. You probably
have no Jewish relatives, am I right?"

"I don't think we do," Karl replied.

"Hitler has convinced the Germans that
the Jews are the cause of all their
problems. He believes that the Germans
are a superior race. And that they should
control the Jews, whom he considers to
be an inferior race. What is amazing is
that the Jews are not even a race. They
are Caucasian, just as you are."

"But why aren't the Jewish people
doing anything?" Karl asked. "If someone
treated me badly, I think I would fight
back."

"Some are trying," Uncle Jacob said,
"but they must be very cautious. The Jews
make up less than one percent of the
population of Germany. And the Nazis are

very powerful. Anyone who causes trouble is either killed or sent to prison."

"But that's terrible," Karl protested.

Uncle Jacob nodded. "Yes, it is," he said. "But it has never been easy for our people. Jews have a long history of persecution. Given time, though, things generally have improved for them. Many of the Jews in Germany believe things will get better. You must remember that there have been Jews in Germany for over 2,000 years. They speak German and are proud to be Germans. They regard Germany as their home. In fact, over 100,000 of them served in the German army during the last war. Many were decorated for bravery. The Jews of Germany can't believe that their fellow citizens would place them in any real danger."

"I didn't realize that the Jews had been in Germany for so long," Karl remarked.

"Oh, yes," Uncle Jacob answered. "And they have produced many great people who have done wonderful things for the country. Poets, writers, musicians, artists. Do you know what the Nobel Prize is, Karl?"

"No," Karl admitted. He'd heard of it but had never been sure what it was.

"The Nobel Prize is awarded every year to five people who have made outstanding achievements in the areas of physics, chemistry, medicine, literature, and peace," Jacob explained. "Did you know, Karl, that of the 38 Nobel Prizes won by German writers and scientists, 14 have gone to Jews?"

Karl shook his head in amazement. How could a government turn against such a worthy group of people? he wondered.

"Enough talk of such things," Aunt Helga interrupted. "This is supposed to be a night of celebration. Let us forget the sadness for an evening and celebrate our good fortune." She looked at Rebecca and raised her glass of lemonade. "To Rebecca's parents' arrival in America!" she said.

"*Prost!*" Uncle Jacob said, using a German toast that meant "cheers." They all raised their glasses.

Karl glanced at Rebecca and was surprised to see tears in her eyes. "Are you all right?" he asked.

Rebecca forced a smile. "I'm fine," she said. "It's just that—I'm worried that something will go wrong. That Mother and Father may not make it to America."

"Of course they will, dear," Aunt Helga assured her. "Everything is arranged. Your parents have visas to get into Cuba and then the United States. They simply have to wait in Cuba until it's their turn to enter the country. What could possibly go wrong?"

"You're right," Rebecca said, wiping her eyes. "I'm just being foolish. What could possibly go wrong?"

As they raised their glasses in another toast, Karl gazed at the remarkable people around him. They're no different from my own family, he thought. They have their weaknesses, and they have their strengths. They agonize over sad things and celebrate happy things. And they cherish their family. Karl took a sip of his lemonade and hoped with all his heart that Rebecca's parents would arrive in America safe and sound.

6 As the school year drew to a close, Karl continued to watch the newspapers and listen to the radio. He knew something had to be wrong in Eastern Europe. Jews were leaving the area by the thousands, the reports said. Ten thousand emigrated to Shanghai. Sixteen thousand went to Palestine. Fifty thousand entered Great Britain.

Many countries were beginning to close their doors to the Jews. Their governments were afraid that the refugees would compete for jobs. And they feared that the Jews would tax the programs set up to assist the needy.

Karl began to worry. How would Cuba feel about the passengers aboard the *S.S. St. Louis* who were headed for its shores? he wondered. And would the U.S. close its doors before Rebecca's parents got in?

On Saturday, May 27, Karl heard what he was dreading. He and his parents were in the living room listening to the news on the radio.

And now for a special report from Cuba, the announcer said. *On Saturday, May 13, the* S.S. St. Louis *left Germany with 936 passengers on board. All but six of them were Jewish. They were headed for Cuba, where they would await entry into the United States.*

"That's the ship Rebecca's parents are on!" Karl cried.

This morning the vessel, owned by Hapag Lines, was not allowed to dock at the company's pier in Havana. Instead they were forced to anchor outside the harbor. Later this morning, Cuban police and immigration officials boarded the St. Louis. *According to witnesses, the immigration officials left shortly after. But police remained on board to ensure that no passengers disembarked.*

Until now, Cuba has had a lenient policy toward refugees. It's not known yet whether the Cuban government has had a change of heart.

Meanwhile, friends and relatives of the passengers rented boats and encircled the St. Louis. *Onlookers said the passengers waved and shouted to those below, but the smaller ships weren't allowed to get close. More later on this story as details develop.*

"I don't understand," Mrs. Schmidt said, turning off the radio. "Why would all those people want to leave Germany?" She picked up her knitting basket and took out the project she was working on—a sweater for Katrina.

"Mom, there's trouble there," Karl said. "Hitler is making it very hard for the Jews."

"But there's trouble everywhere, Karl," his mother said as her needles clicked away. "Do you think it wasn't hard for the Irish when they first came to America? But you didn't see them running back to Ireland."

Karl was getting frustrated. "Mom, the Nazis have passed laws making the Jews second-class citizens."

"Well, if I remember my history, the Irish were treated that way here too," Mrs. Schmidt said. "But eventually things got better for them."

"But the Jews have been in Germany for generations, Mom," Karl said. "Things are getting worse for them instead of better. And they're leaving the country by the thousands. Hitler is—" he turned to his father for help. "Dad, tell her about Hitler."

Mr. Schmidt started to speak, but Mrs. Schmidt cut him off. "Your father and I have already had this discussion, dear. He and I don't see eye to eye on Germany's new leader." She shook her head then and laid her knitting in her lap. "No, it's the Jews' choice if they want to leave the country," she said. "But personally, I think they're being foolish. Hitler is doing great things for Germany, and sooner or later they'll benefit from them. In my mind, they're simply being too impatient. Why, I just received another letter from Berta yesterday. She can't say enough good things about the new government."

Karl sighed. How could he make her understand? She refused to believe that anything bad was going on in Germany. But then who could blame her? he thought. She only knew one side of the story—the side she got from Berta's letters. They had no Jewish relatives in Germany to write and tell her their side.

Karl shook his head. People only notice what affects them, he thought. As long as it happens to the other guy, it's none of their concern. It would take something bad to happen to her sister's family to wake his mother up to reality. And since Berta and the others were what the Nazis considered "true Aryans," that probably wasn't going to happen any time soon.

* * *

On Sunday Karl called Rebecca. "Are you all right?" he asked. "I heard the report about the *St. Louis* last night."

"Oh, Karl, I'm so worried," Rebecca said. "I was afraid something like this would happen."

"Have you heard anything more?" Karl wanted to know.

"No," Rebecca said miserably. "Uncle Jacob is keeping the radio on all day, though, in case there's more news."

Karl could hear the anguish in her voice. He *had* to say something to make her feel better. "Look, Rebecca, things could still turn out all right," he said. "Maybe the Cuban government is just making sure everything is in order before they let the passengers off. You know how much red tape there is whenever the government's involved. It's not time to worry yet."

"That's what Uncle Jacob says," Rebecca replied. "But I don't think I'll stop worrying until I see my parents walk through the door of this house."

* * *

The next week was the last week of school. Karl faced the end of the year with mixed feelings. He was glad to be done with another year of schooling. But he was a little nervous about the next fall when he would be a senior. He still had no idea what he wanted to do with his life. Although lately he realized that he was developing an interest in history, something that had never really appealed to him before.

Since the incident with the *S.S. St. Louis* had begun, Karl had spent most evenings at the Silvermans' house. Aunt Helga would bring them all refreshments. Then they would huddle around the radio, waiting for any news about the fate of the passengers.

Those evenings had led to long talks with Uncle Jacob about history. Uncle Jacob usually began the talks. But he always drew Karl, as well as Rebecca and Aunt Helga, into the conversation. After a few nights, Karl realized that it was an attempt on the older man's part to get the group's minds off what was happening in Cuba.

The more Karl talked to Uncle Jacob, the more he realized that the man was a true scholar. Not only did he know about European history. But also he was an expert on ancient civilization. He had written a book about the "cradle of civilization" in western Asia. He told Karl that this area was where historians believed civilization had begun.

Uncle Jacob lent Karl a copy of his book. "Summer reading material," he had said, smiling.

Karl had taken the huge volume with reservation. He'd never been much of a reader. But that night he'd had trouble falling asleep. So about 11:30 he opened the book and began reading. When Karl looked at the clock again, it was 2:30 in the morning. Now every night he looked forward to an hour of reading at bedtime. He found the book fascinating and planned on asking Uncle Jacob if he could borrow other books from his extensive library.

One night as the four were discussing the events of the Great War, Aunt Helga suddenly reached over and turned up the volume on the radio. "Shh!" she said, holding up her hand. "There's something on about the *St. Louis!*"

Karl held his breath. The last they had heard, the ship was still docked outside of Havana, waiting for word from the Cuban government. He reached over and took Rebecca's hand. In silence, they all stared straight at the radio.

The world continues to watch the fate of the passengers on board the S.S. St. Louis, the announcer said. *The latest news is that there has been an attempted suicide. Some time after dark, a male passenger jumped overboard. Onlookers say the man slit his wrists right before jumping.*

A courageous crew member jumped into the water to save him. Witnesses report that the man was struggling against his rescuer, screaming "I won't go back! I won't go back! They'll arrest us all!" The disturbance drew police boats to the area. After putting up a fight, the man was pushed into a police boat by the crew member. Relatives on shore identified the man as Max Loewe, a Jew from Frankfurt. They speculate that Loewe had become increasingly despondent over the delayed departure of the passengers. The St. Louis *has been docked just outside the harbor now for four days as negotiations for its passengers' entry into the country continue.*

"How awful," Aunt Helga said. "That poor man."

Karl looked at Rebecca. She sat perfectly still with her eyes closed. He squeezed her hand, and she clasped his tighter.

As a result of the incident, the number of police boats in the harbor has been increased, the announcer continued.

Searchlights have been installed to scan the ship. And lights have been set up all over the harbor to illuminate the water. Fearing more suicides, the Cubans are intent on discouraging any other passengers from jumping overboard. Now on to other news.

Aunt Helga reached over and turned down the radio. For a few moments they sat in stunned silence. Finally Rebecca burst into tears. "What will happen to them?" she sobbed.

Karl put his arm around her shoulders. "Rebecca, it's not time to worry yet," he said. "Your parents are safe on board the ship. Things could change at any time. By tomorrow they could be in Cuba."

"But what if they're not?" Rebecca cried. "What if the Cubans never let them in and send them back—" her voice dropped to a whisper "—to Germany!"

"Surely that won't happen—will it, Jacob?" Aunt Helga said. Karl could hear worry in her words.

"Of course not," Uncle Jacob said confidently. "There are plenty of other places the boat can go if that happens.

Perhaps if Cuba won't take them, the United States will. Cuba is only a short distance from Florida, after all. And the passengers already have visas to get into this country." He looked at his niece and smiled. "Think of it, Rebecca. If that happens, your parents could be here sooner than expected!"

Rebecca nodded and smiled bravely. Karl continued to hold her hand. He glanced at Uncle Jacob. The older man's mouth was fixed in a smile, but his eyes were full of worry.

7 The last day of school was only a half-day, so Karl took Rebecca to the lake for an afternoon of swimming. It was warm for the beginning of June—92 degrees. Karl thought it was a perfect day to spend at the beach. And he wanted to provide Rebecca with a diversion to take her mind off her parents' predicament.

"Race you to the water!" Karl yelled after they had spread out their towels on the beach.

They both ran laughing into the lake.

"This reminds me of a lake back home," Rebecca said as she floated on her back next to Karl. "Only that lake was prettier. It was surrounded by mountains. And the water was so clear, you could see to the bottom."

"Mmm, sounds nice," Karl said, closing his eyes and enjoying the warmth of the sun on his face.

"It was," Rebecca replied wistfully. "Oh, Karl, Germany is such a beautiful country! It makes me sad to think I may never go back."

"Don't say that, Rebecca," Karl said. "You might go back someday."

"Do you think that could really happen, Karl?" Rebecca asked.

"Sure. Sooner or later, the German people are going to figure out what kind of maniac Hitler is," Karl said. "When that happens, the government will change. And then the Jews will return. As your Uncle Jacob said, it's been their home for 2,000 years. They belong there."

"I hope you're right, Karl," Rebecca said.

The afternoon passed quickly. At about 4:00, Karl noticed that the sun was getting low in the sky. But he didn't want to take Rebecca home yet. He liked being with her. And he wanted to keep her mind off her parents for as long as possible.

"Hey, how about we stop at the drugstore for a root beer float?" he suggested.

"I'd like that," Rebecca replied.

At the drugstore, they each ordered super-deluxe root beer floats in honor of their first "date."

"Remember the first time I brought you here?" Karl asked as they waited for their orders.

Rebecca laughed. "Yes, you were so shy," she said. "You hardly knew what to say."

Karl smiled. "Well, at least I don't have that problem anymore," he said. "You know, Rebecca, you're one of the easiest girls to talk to that I've ever met."

"Maybe that's because I like talking to you," Rebecca said.

Their order came then, and they sipped in silence for a few minutes. Karl could hear a radio playing softly behind the counter. The clerk was at the other end of the counter wiping it down with a damp cloth. Suddenly he stopped and turned up the radio.

Reports have been confirmed, the announcer was saying. The crew and passengers of the S.S. St. Louis *have been ordered to leave Cuban waters. Efforts are being made to continue negotiations. However, for now the* St. Louis *must leave Cuba. According to one official, if the ship does not leave peacefully, it will be forced out by the Cuban navy.*

Rebecca gasped and covered her mouth with her hand, knocking over her glass.

The clerk turned down the volume on the radio and hurried over to wipe up the spill. As he worked, he shook his head and said, "Those poor people. You have to feel sorry for them, don't you?"

Karl felt sick. What Rebecca had dreaded most had actually happened. What would happen to her parents now?

* * *

For several days as negotiations continued, the captain of the *St. Louis* circled Cuba. On one evening, the ship headed north to the coast of Florida. The boat came so close to the Florida coast that the people on board could see the lights of Miami. The captain radioed the Coast Guard, asking that the United States accept the passengers. But the captain's appeals for help were futile. His ship was not allowed to dock. And Coast Guard ships patrolled the water to make sure no one jumped to freedom.

Then on Tuesday, June 6, the president of Cuba closed the negotiations. The passengers would not be allowed to enter his country. The next day, the *St. Louis* headed back to Germany.

The mood was somber in the Silvermans' living room that evening. Uncle Jacob sat quietly, pulling on his beard. Aunt Helga leafed through a magazine, sighing with every turn of a page. And Rebecca and Karl sat silently on the sofa, holding hands. Finally, Karl spoke.

"What will happen now?" he asked Uncle Jacob.

"Negotiations are underway with other countries to take the passengers," he said.

"Do you think that will happen?" Karl asked.

Uncle Jacob shook his head and said, "Honestly, Karl, I don't know. I thought the United States would have taken them in." He was silent for a moment. Then he burst out, "Curse the immigration quotas! We're dealing with peoples' lives here!"

Aunt Helga went to him then and placed her hand on his shoulder. "We must not give up hope, Jacob," she said.

Uncle Jacob turned his head sideways and brushed her hand with his lips.

"You're right, my dear," he said. "There is still hope. Surely another country will be merciful and take them in."

* * *

When Karl got home that evening, his parents were in the living room.

"How are the Silvermans holding up?" Mr. Schmidt asked as Karl sat down on the couch beside him.

"About as well as can be expected, I guess," Karl said. "They're waiting to find out if any other countries will take the passengers from the *St. Louis*."

"I hope so," Mr. Schmidt said. "Those people have been through enough. Someone needs to show them some compassion."

"It wouldn't be the worst thing in the world if they were taken back to Germany," Mrs. Schmidt said.

"Yes, it would, Mom," Karl insisted. "They're arresting people left and right there."

"They only arrest troublemakers, I'm sure," Mrs. Schmidt replied. "If those people just stay out of trouble—"

"Mom, they tried to *leave Germany!*" Karl cried. "Don't you think the Nazis would consider them troublemakers for that? They can't go back. Don't you see?"

"Calm down, Karl," Mr. Schmidt said. "Your mother is entitled to her opinion too. It doesn't do any good to yell."

"I'm sorry, Mom," Karl said. "I just don't think you realize what's going on over there. You only get Berta's side of the story."

"That's true," Mrs. Schmidt said. "But at the same time, Karl, you're only listening to the Silvermans' side. I can't imagine that things can be as bad as the Silvermans say."

"Look at it this way, son," Mr. Schmidt said. "The whole world has been watching this ordeal. If those passengers go back to Germany, the Nazis wouldn't dare touch them. Everyone would know about it."

"Maybe you're right," Karl said. In any case, he was tired of arguing about it. He decided to go to bed. "Well, goodnight."

"Goodnight, Karl," his parents said.

As Karl headed up the stairs to his

bedroom, he thought about what his dad had just said. The world had been watching when the Germans marched into Austria. And it was watching when they took over Czechoslovakia. Why would anyone think the Germans cared who was watching when the passengers from the *S.S. St. Louis* returned?

* * *

A few days later, Rebecca called with good news. "Karl, we just received a telegram from my parents! Four countries have agreed to take the passengers!" she exclaimed.

Karl breathed a huge sigh of relief. "Oh, man, that's great, Rebecca," he said. "Which countries?"

"Holland, France, Great Britain, and Belgium," Rebecca answered. "Oh, Karl, I'm so relieved!"

"I know. Me too," Karl said. "Did your parents say where they will go?"

"Yes, to Belgium," Rebecca said. "We have relatives in Antwerp. They're going to meet my parents when the boat docks.

Mother and Father will stay with them until they can decide what to do." Then she sighed. "It makes me sad that I won't see them as planned, but they're safe. And that's all that matters."

"That's right," Karl said. "That's all that matters."

"Of course, Aunt Helga wants to have another celebration," Rebecca said. "This evening at 6:00. Can you come?"

"I wouldn't miss it," Karl replied.

8 The summer passed quickly after that. Karl's dad managed to get him a part-time job sorting mail at the post office. It was only a few hours a week, but it gave Karl spending money to take Rebecca out.

At least once a week, the two went to a movie or on some kind of outing. Saturdays Rebecca stayed home to observe the Sabbath with her aunt and uncle. And every Sunday afternoon Karl accompanied the Silvermans to the band concert in the park. There the Westphalia town band played German songs while the townspeople sat on blankets and ate picnic lunches.

One Sunday as they sat listening to a German polka, Karl looked at the crowd around him. A few blankets away Mr. Wagner sat with David Hummel's sister. Beside them sat David and his ever-present friend, Stephen. Mr. Wagner, Stephen, and David had their heads together and were talking quietly. Karl wondered what the three were talking about. He noticed that occasionally one of them would glance toward the

Silvermans. But as soon as they met Karl's eyes, they glanced away. Though he couldn't say why, the presence of the three bothered Karl. He kept an eye on them for a few more minutes. But they soon stopped talking and sat quietly, listening to the band. After a while Karl forgot they were there.

He had other things to think about, like how happy he was. He glanced at the people beside him. Uncle Jacob, surely one of the most knowledgeable people he had ever met. Aunt Helga, a gracious and refined woman of many talents. And Rebecca, a beautiful and intelligent girl who still amazed him. Karl couldn't remember ever being so content with his life.

But things changed before the summer was over. Late in August, Aunt Helga received another letter from The Anonymous Aryan. "Flee!" it warned. "Flee from your sinful marriage before the wrath of Hitler is upon you!"

This time the Silvermans reported the letter to the police. But the police could do nothing without more evidence. They assured Uncle Jacob and Aunt Helga that the letter was probably a hoax and that nothing would come of it.

The second dark spot of the summer occurred just days before school began. On Friday, September 1, Hitler shocked the world when his armies crashed across the borders of Poland.

Karl was just leaving with Rebecca for a final outing to the beach when Uncle Jacob came running out the door. "Quick! Come listen! The Germans are marching on Poland!"

The four took their traditional places in front of the radio and listened.

We repeat: German troops have invaded Poland, the announcer said. *The Germans have started their attack from the air.* Stuka *dive bombers are blasting Polish planes on the ground. They're targeting railroads, bridges, and highways. And they're said to be headed toward Warsaw and other major cities. Citizens there have been warned to seek shelter. We repeat: German troops have invaded Poland.*

"What does this mean, Uncle Jacob?"

Rebecca asked, her eyes wide and fearful.

Uncle Jacob pulled on his beard before speaking. "I'm afraid it means war, Rebecca," Uncle Jacob replied.

"What do you mean?" Karl asked.

"Many have suspected that Hitler has had his eye on Poland for a long time," Uncle Jacob explained. "France was so sure of it that it signed a treaty with Poland to protect it from invasion. So did Great Britain. Surely, both countries will now declare war on Germany."

Uncle Jacob was right. Two days later, on September 3, 1939, Great Britain and France declared war on Germany. And a darkness descended on Europe as another world war began.

* * *

A few days later school started. As Karl walked toward Westphalia High, he noticed a cool dryness to the air. A sure sign of fall, he thought.

For the most part, he was pleased with his classes. He'd gotten Mrs. Fields for senior English. He'd had her for

composition when he was a sophomore
and had liked her. And he had Miss
Marsch again for Latin. He'd always
gotten along well with her. He read the
rest of his schedule. Mr. Clarke for
chemistry. That was okay. Mr. Clarke had
a reputation for being tough but fair. Mrs.
Anderson, the new teacher, for math. He
hoped she was nice.

The only teacher Karl was unhappy
with was Mr. Wagner. Besides American
history, Mr. Wagner taught government.
All seniors were required to take this
course.

Karl wondered if Rebecca would be in
his class. In a way he wanted her to be,
and in another way he didn't. He always
welcomed the chance to be in the same
room with her. But he didn't like to think
that he might have to witness Mr.
Wagner's treatment of her again. Then
again, he thought, maybe the teacher had
changed over the summer. He'd heard that
Mr. Wagner had married David Hummel's
sister. Marriage can change a person, Karl
thought. Maybe he's more considerate of
others now.

Karl didn't see Rebecca until third period. As it turned out, she was in his government class. He took a seat right across from her and smiled.

"Hi," he said.

"Hello, Karl," Rebecca said quietly.

Karl could tell she was tense about being there. "You okay?" he asked.

"I guess," Rebecca said, managing a small smile. "I just hope this semester goes by quickly."

"It will," Karl assured her. He glanced around the room. Most of the same kids from American history were there—including Stephen Franks and David Hummel. As usual, Stephen and David were together. Two peas in a pod, Karl thought. But then he looked closer at them. They were more alike than usual. Each of them wore a dark brown shirt and black trousers. Underneath the cuffs of their pants, Karl could see heavy, black boots. Their clothing looked uniform-like. And on their desks lay their notebooks— each decorated with a bold, black swastika.

He glanced at Rebecca. She was staring

at them too. "Karl," she whispered. "Stephen and David—look how they're dressed!"

Suddenly Karl realized where he had seen such clothing before. It was the uniform of the Hitler Youth. His cousin Josef had been wearing those same clothes in the picture Berta had sent. The only difference was, Josef had worn shorts. It was against the school dress code to wear shorts, however, so Stephen and David had opted for trousers.

Just then Mr. Wagner walked into the room. *"Guten Morgen, Klasse!"* he said.

"Good morning, Mr. Wagner," the class answered.

"Herr Vag-ner," the teacher said.

A few of the students glanced sideways at each other.

Why would Mr. Wagner want students to use the German pronunciation of his name this year? Karl wondered. And why would he want to be called *Herr* instead of Mr.? He looked at Rebecca. She looked very uncomfortable.

"Guten Morgen, Herr Wagner," a few students said, led by Stephen and David.

"So! We begin a new year together," Mr. Wagner went on. "I trust you all had pleasant summers, *ja?*"

Many of the students nodded their heads.

"*Gut! Gut!*" Mr. Wagner said. "For now it is time to get to work. As you know, this is government class. That means that this semester we will be looking closely at the American form of government, democracy. We'll be examining how the government is structured and how it works. We will be looking at its strengths—and its obvious weaknesses. But, as in all my classes, we will start out the hour each day with a brief discussion of current events."

Immediately David's hand shot in the air. "Last week Germany invaded Poland!" he said. Karl heard a note of triumph in David's voice.

"That's right, David," Mr. Wagner said. "And then?" he looked around the room.

"France and Great Britain declared war on Germany," Klaus Wesson said.

"What will happen now, Mr. Wagner?" Heidi asked.

"*Herr Vagner,*" Mr. Wagner corrected her. "Poland will most certainly fall."

"Yeah, Poland doesn't stand a chance against *Blitzkrieg,*" Stephen said.

"What's *Blitzkrieg?*" another student asked.

"Lighting war!" Stephen said.

"What does that mean?" Klaus asked.

"*Blitzkrieg* is a new kind of warfare the Germans are using. It involves a series of rapid attacks by aircraft and armor," Mr. Wagner explained. "The Germans begin the attack just as they did in Poland—from the air. They send in *Stuka* dive bombers first. The pilots bomb key communication points such as highways and bridges."

"I heard the bombers have sirens on them to make them sound more terrifying to the people below," David said.

"*Ja.* Ingenious, isn't it?" Mr. Wagner replied. "After the dive bombers 'soften up' the enemy, the ground forces move in— the soldiers on motorcycles, the tanks. They prepare the way for the foot soldiers, who finish the job."

"Is it true that Russia is attacking Poland too?" Heidi asked.

"Yes, they are advancing from the east. The Germans, from the west," Mr. Wagner answered.

"Like I said, the Poles don't stand a chance," Stephen laughed.

"Will the United States get into the war, *Herr* Wagner?" Klaus wanted to know.

"It doesn't look like it," the teacher answered. "The U.S. is following a policy of isolationism. Which means they are avoiding getting involved in things that go on overseas. The American people don't want another war.

"All right, that's enough discussion for now," he said, moving to the back of the room and opening a metal cabinet. "Let's begin passing out books."

"Mr.—*Herr* Wagner," Heidi said.

"Yes, Heidi?" the teacher replied as he removed the textbooks.

"What will happen to the people in Poland if they are conquered by the Germans?" Heidi wanted to know.

With a stack of books in his arms, Mr. Wagner turned around and faced the class. "It depends on what kind of people they are, Heidi," he said as he began passing out books. "If they are Aryans, their lives will probably go on as usual. If they are non-Aryans," he shrugged, "who knows? They will probably be put to work for the good of the German empire. After all, the Germans are the conquerors. They can do whatever they like with the spoils of war."

Empire? Karl thought. Since when was Germany an empire? An empire indicated control of a huge area of land. So far Germany had only two small countries—Austria and Czechoslovakia. And now possibly Poland. The Germans would have to conquer many more countries to call themselves an empire. Mr. Wagner was exaggerating, Karl decided. Then he had a disturbing thought. Perhaps Mr. Wagner was being optimistic.

9 That afternoon, Karl went home, expecting his mother to greet him at the door. As always, she would be anxious to hear about his first day of school. But today, Karl saw no sign of his mother as he walked into the house. He set his books down on the kitchen table and moved from room to room looking for her. Finally he found her in the bedroom. She was holding a piece of paper in her hand and crying into a handkerchief.

Karl had never seen his mother cry before except at funerals. He knew something terrible had happened.

"Mom, what's the matter?" Karl asked, sitting on the bed beside her.

Mrs. Schmidt was sobbing so hard she could hardly speak. She waved the letter in the air toward Karl. "It's Berta's husband. Emil—he's been arrested!"

"What?" Karl cried.

But Mrs. Schmidt just shook her head and handed him the letter.

Karl took the letter and recognized Berta's neat handwriting. He read:

Dear Johanna,

I have most distressing news. Emil

has been arrested and taken to prison.

In shock, Karl looked at his mother. "What did he do?" he asked. But Mrs. Schmidt just covered her mouth with her handkerchief and sobbed more. Karl read on.

Do you remember my telling you how Emil has always been against Josef's activities in the Jungvolk? *Last week he demanded that Josef withdraw from the organization, but Josef refused. Josef mentioned his father's objections to his group leader. That night, the German police came to our home and took Emil away. He is being held in jail right now. They cannot tell me for how long.*

Please try to understand, Johanna. Josef was only doing his duty. I cannot blame him. He did what we have all been instructed to do. To report anyone who might stand in the way of Germany's goals. The Jungvolk *are an important part of Germany. They are its future leaders. Everyone agrees that no opportunities should be denied them.*

And they are such fine young people, Johanna. I wish you could see the parades they march in. Hundreds of boys and girls carrying flags in honor of our glorious leader. And thousands upon thousands of Germans saluting them and cheering them on.

While I grieve for my husband, I am proud of my son for showing the depth of his loyalty to his country. As soon as I know something more about Emil, I will write again. With love to you and yours. Heil Hitler!

Berta

Karl couldn't believe what he had just read. Josef had ratted on his own father! How could any son do such a thing? And Berta saw nothing wrong with it! Was Hitler brainwashing the German people? he wondered.

"Oh, Karl," Mrs. Schmidt sobbed. "You were right! You've been right all along! Hitler must be a very evil man to encourage such behavior from a child. I realize that now."

"That's what I've been trying to tell you, Mom," Karl said. "If Hitler does things like that to his own people, think what he does to those he considers inferior!"

"I know, I know," his mother said. "I'm so sorry, Karl. I should have listened to you and your father. But I so wanted things to be better for my sister and her family."

"I know, Mom," Karl said. "But you can't make things better for one group by making them worse for another. And that's what Hitler's doing."

Mrs. Schmidt blew her nose. "It's crazy," she said, shaking her head. "Hitler must be a madman."

"I think so too," Karl agreed. "And something has to be done to stop him. I only hope the French and British can do it!"

But despite the treaties France and Britain had made, they were unable to protect Poland. In only three weeks, the country fell to the Germans. The whole world was shocked and wondered which country the Nazis would try for next.

Rebecca began to worry about her parents' safety. "Belgium is right next to Germany, Karl. And it's such a tiny country. What will happen to my parents if the Germans invade it?"

Karl tried to say something to comfort her. "Rebecca, other countries will join France and Great Britain if that happens. They won't let Germany get away with taking another country."

"I hope you're right, Karl," Rebecca said.

"I *know* I'm right," Karl said. But he hoped he sounded more convinced than he felt.

* * *

At the end of September, Mrs. Fields, Karl's English teacher, announced that they were beginning a novel unit. "We'll be reading a book that's new to the curriculum, class. It's called *The Call of the Wild* by Jack London," Mrs. Fields said.

Karl smiled. That was the book Rebecca's Uncle Jacob had recommended. Karl remembered that Uncle Jacob had said it was about a dog.

The first night the class was to read chapters 1 and 2. Karl didn't have time to finish all of chapter 2. So he carried the book to government class with him the next morning. Sometimes Mr. Wagner allowed them a few free minutes at the end of the period. Karl thought he could read the last few pages then.

Just as Karl hoped, Mr. Wagner finished the lesson ten minutes before the bell rang. "*Klasse*, you may have the rest of the period to study. *Stille!*"

Karl took out the novel and opened it. He had just started reading when a shadow fell across the pages. Looking up, he saw Mr. Wagner standing over him. The teacher had a frown on his face.

"*Vas ist* that book?" Mr. Wagner asked. Karl noticed that he spoke more and more with a German accent.

"It's *The Call of the Wild*, sir," Karl replied.

"Since *ven ist* such drivel taught here at *Vestphalia* High?" the teacher demanded.

"Mrs. Fields said it's a new book this year," Karl explained. He wondered why Mr. Wagner was taking such an interest in his book.

Mr. Wagner picked up the book. "*Und* who else is reading this?" he asked.

Several students raised their hands.

"You *vill* not read this book in my *Klassenzimmer* again!" the teacher commanded.

"But why not, *Herr* Wagner?" Heidi asked. She was one who had raised her hand.

"Jack London writes subversive books," Mr. Wagner said. "His *vorks* teach people the wrong things."

"But the main character is a dog, sir," Karl pointed out as politely as he could.

"*Stille!* It doesn't matter!" Mr. Wagner almost shouted. "The story promotes self-indulgence. It encourages people to care more about their own *velfare* than the *velfare* of their country. Of their government. These kinds of ideas lead to defiance and revolt!"

"But—" Karl began.

"Enough!" Mr. Wagner insisted. "None of you *vill* read that book in my classroom again. And you can be sure I *vill* be talking to Mrs. Fields about removing it from the course of study!"

Stephen and David obediently closed their books and put them away. The others looked confused for a minute.

Then they did the same.

When the bell rang, Karl walked Rebecca to her locker. "Man, what got into him?" he asked.

"Don't you remember, Karl?" Rebecca said. "Uncle Jacob told us that Jack London's novels were some of those destroyed in the book burnings in Germany."

"Oh, gosh, that's right," Karl said, remembering now. Suddenly it was starting to add up. Mr. Wagner's unfair treatment of Rebecca, the only Jewish student in the class. The experiment he conducted to show the difference between Aryans and non-Aryans. His insistence on being called *Herr Vagner.* His increased use of German in his speech and his heavy German accent. His defense of Germany. "Rebecca, do you think Mr. Wagner is a —"

"Nazi?" Rebecca said. "I *know* so."

"But how?" Karl asked.

"I walked by his desk this morning as he was opening his drawer," Rebecca began. "He had a copy of *Mein Kampf* in his drawer."

"*Mein Kampf?*" Karl repeated. "What's that?"

"A book by Adolf Hitler," Rebecca explained. "It means 'my struggle.' "

"So?" Karl asked.

"Hitler wrote it when he was imprisoned for trying to overthrow the government of Bavaria," Rebecca replied.

"Bavaria? Isn't that part of Germany?" Karl wanted to know.

Rebecca nodded and said, "Yes, it's like a state. Anyway, his revolt failed, and he was sent to prison for nine months. During that time he wrote *Mein Kampf*. The book is filled with anti-Jewish propaganda. It's about power worship—and it explains Hitler's plans to take over the world! Don't you see, Karl? *Mein Kampf* is the bible of the Nazi party!"

"Rebecca, something has to be done about Wagner," Karl said. "Before he becomes dangerous. Would you be willing to go to the principal's office with me after school and tell her about it? Maybe she can do something?"

"If you think it will help, Karl," Rebecca

replied. "But I doubt that there's a law against what Mr. Wagner reads."

"Maybe not," Karl said. "But I think Mrs. Wasserman should at least be aware of what's going on. I'll meet you by your locker after school. See you then."

"Good-bye, Karl," Rebecca said.

Mrs. Wasserman was a pleasant woman of about 55. She was a firm disciplinarian who allowed no nonsense at Westphalia High. But she was also very supportive of the students. And she encouraged the faculty to view each student as an individual of worth.

But as Rebecca predicted, Mrs. Wasserman could not offer much help as far as Mr. Wagner was concerned. The two gave her the details of what they had observed. Then Mrs. Wasserman said, "I'm very disturbed by what is going on in Germany. I think Adolf Hitler is a dangerous man whose actions will bring more harm to Germany than good. But there is no law against Mr. Wagner supporting the beliefs of Nazism. Or joining the Nazi party, for that matter. This is a democracy, and people are free to do as they choose. However, what he did to you that day in class, Rebecca, was not right. I'll talk to him about it and see that such 'experiments' don't occur again."

"With all due respect, Mrs. Wasserman, I'd rather you didn't," Rebecca said.

Mrs. Wasserman raised her eyebrows and said, "Oh?"

"I'm afraid Mr. Wagner will make things harder for me," Rebecca explained. "I just want to get through the semester without any more trouble."

"I understand," Mrs. Wasserman replied. "And I will honor your wishes. However, should something like that occur again, I want to know about it. Mr. Wagner might have the right to be a Nazi if he chooses. But he does *not* have the right to humiliate any of the students here at Westphalia High. Thank you both for coming in today."

"Thank you, Mrs. Wasserman," Karl said. The two left the building and started home.

"I'm glad we went, aren't you?" Karl asked as they walked.

Rebecca nodded and said, "Mrs.

Wasserman is a good person. I feel better just knowing that she's aware of Mr. Wagner's attitude. At least she can keep an eye on him."

"Have you said anything to your aunt and uncle about all this?" Karl asked.

"Oh, no, Karl," Rebecca said quickly. She grabbed his arm. "And don't you say anything either. They have enough to worry about. My parents being in Belgium. And those horrible letters. I don't want them to have to worry about me too. They've been so wonderful to open up their home to me. I don't want to cause them any pain."

"Okay, I won't," Karl promised, moving his arm to take her by the hand. "Has your aunt received any more letters?"

Rebecca shook her head. "No, thank goodness," she said.

"Well, the police were probably right," Karl assured her. "Those letters were probably just a hoax."

10 Three days later, Aunt Helga received her third letter from The Anonymous Aryan. *Flee! Flee this abomination you call a marriage!* it read. *You defile the Fürher's name and the name of all Germans! Flee or you will be sorry!*

Once again, the Silvermans were told that there was nothing the police could do. The police chief only promised that a squad car would patrol their neighborhood closely for the next few days.

A week later, Karl was in the Silvermans' living room listening to Aunt Helga play the piano. As usual, Rebecca was sitting next to him. Uncle Jacob sat in his rocking chair by the window, leafing through a book.

Aunt Helga was playing the beautiful "Blue Danube" waltz. Karl was awed by her playing. As Rebecca had said, she was a skilled pianist. For Karl, she made the waltz come alive. He could almost see the great blue river as it wove its way through Europe.

Suddenly a great shattering of glass

broke the serenity of the room. Aunt Helga shrieked, and her playing ended abruptly in a jarring chord. Karl looked up to see Uncle Jacob slump in his chair and then tumble out. Blood quickly soaked the tapestry rug under his head. At the same time, a large rock bounced across the floor toward Karl. Automatically, Karl picked it up. The words *Jew Lover* were scrawled across one side of the rock.

"Uncle!" Rebecca screamed. Immediately she and Aunt Helga were by the injured man's side.

"Quick! We must stop the bleeding!" Aunt Helga cried. "Karl! Run to the kitchen. Grab every towel you can find!"

Karl ran to the kitchen and began opening every drawer and cabinet. He found a stack of hand towels and raced back to the living room. He gave the towels to Aunt Helga, who gently wrapped one around Uncle Jacob's head. Rebecca loosened the collar of Uncle Jacob's shirt. Karl could see that Uncle Jacob's face was pale and that his mouth hung slack. He was obviously unconscious.

Aunt Helga spoke calmly to Karl. "Karl,"

she said, "use the telephone to call the hospital. See if they will send an ambulance."

Karl walked to the phone in a daze. He couldn't believe what was happening. Why would anyone want to hurt gentle and intelligent Jacob Silverman? he wondered. Somehow he managed to phone the hospital. They told him they would send an ambulance. Then he returned to the living room.

Karl stood helplessly by watching the two women hovering over Uncle Jacob. Slowly he became aware of a reflection of flashing lights on the walls around him. He knew it was too soon for the ambulance. He wondered if the police had heard the disturbance and had arrived at the Silvermans' house. He thought maybe the flashing reflection was the red light of a squad car. Karl stood there a minute longer, expecting the police to knock on the door. But no knock came.

Karl glanced at the reflection again. Suddenly he realized that the flashing lights were the flames of a fire. He ran to the window and looked out. There on the Silvermans' lawn stood a burning cross.

In a panic, Karl searched his mind. Who had done this? Where had he heard of burning crosses recently? He knew that the Ku Klux Klan had often burned crosses at the churches or in the yards of black people. But this had been more recent. His mind raced as he grasped for an answer. Finally he remembered! Rebecca had told him that crosses were being burned on the lawns of "undesirables" in Germany. The Anonymous Aryan! It had to be! He was trying to scare Aunt Helga into leaving Uncle Jacob.

A few seconds later, a police car screeched to a halt in front of the Silvermans' house. A policeman got out of the car and hurried across the Silvermans' lawn. He slowed down to glance at the burning cross. Then he continued on. Soon Karl heard a loud, sharp knocking at the door.

"Mr. Silverman? Mrs. Silverman? Are you folks okay?" a man called, his voice coming through the broken window.

Karl went to the door and let the policeman in. "Are you okay?" the policeman asked again.

"This way," Karl said. He led the man into the living room. There on the floor lay Uncle Jacob. Aunt Helga held his injured head in her lap and stroked his face. Blood slowly seeped from the wound onto the skirt of her dress. Rebecca knelt beside them, praying.

The policeman hurried to their side. He checked Uncle Jacob's breathing and pulse. "His vital signs are good," he said. "Has an ambulance been sent for?"

"Yes," Aunt Helga said. She continued to stroke her husband's face.

"Come here, son," the policeman said. He led Karl outside to speak in private. Numbly, Karl followed. The cross still burned brightly on the lawn. It held his gaze as the policeman spoke to him.

"Are you a family member?" the policeman asked.

Karl shook his head. He could not have spoken if he'd wanted to. A man he loved dearly lay injured on the floor. And why? Because someone had determined that

Uncle Jacob should be punished for his religion. How many people over the centuries had been punished, even killed, because of their religion? Karl wondered. Thousands, maybe even millions. It didn't make sense. Why should someone be punished for the way he viewed God?

Karl was brought out of his reverie by the sound of the policeman's voice.

"Well, you'll be happy to know we got the people who did this," the policeman was saying. "My partner and I were cruising by when we saw three men running through the next yard, heading for the alley. We apprehended them. They're out in the squad car now. They'll pay plenty for this."

Karl glanced toward the squad car. In the light cast by the flames of the burning cross, Karl could see Mr. Wagner in the back seat. Beside him sat David Hummel and Stephen Franks.

"Any idea who those wise guys are?" the policeman asked.

Karl shook his head. I used to know them, he thought. Mr. Wagner was a tough but dedicated teacher of American history. As with all teachers, some kids liked him and some didn't. Stephen Franks and David Hummel were two regular kids who'd grown up with Karl. They had been in the same Boy Scout troop and belonged to Karl's church.

All three of the people in the back seat of the squad car had been born and raised in the United States. And all three had been taught the American ideals of freedom and individualism. But somewhere along the line they'd changed. At some point they had gotten the idea into their heads that they were better than others. And that it was their duty to control those they considered inferior.

"Son, I asked you if you had any idea who these fellows are?" the policeman repeated.

Karl shook his head again. "I thought I did," he replied sadly. "But not anymore."

Albert Wagner was fined $100 for criminal mischief. A month later, he and his new wife left the country. It was rumored in Westphalia that he had gone to Germany to join the Nazi forces.

David Hummel admitted to throwing the rock that injured Jacob Silverman. He received two years at a boys' reformatory school. Stephen Franks, for his part in the crime, served one year at the school. Evidently, both boys were reformed. For upon their release, they joined the United States Army and fought valiantly against the Germans.

Uncle Jacob survived with only a concussion. He and Aunt Helga lived happily in Westphalia for the rest of their lives.

All did not go as well for Jacob's brother and his wife. In the spring of 1940, the German army stormed through Europe, conquering Denmark, Norway, Luxembourg, Holland—and Belgium where Rebecca's parents were. Dr. and Mrs. Silverman died two years later in a concentration camp in 1943. It was later discovered that the Nazis had spread rumors in Cuba that the Jews aboard the *S.S. St. Louis* were dangerous criminals. These rumors reached the president of

Cuba, causing him to refuse the passengers entry into his country.

In December of 1941, the United States joined the war when the Japanese attacked Pearl Harbor. Along with the Germans, the Japanese were trying to conquer the world.

Karl joined the army and fought against the Japanese in the South Pacific. When he returned to Westphalia in 1945, Rebecca was waiting, and the two were married. Karl later went on to become a historian who specialized in Jewish history. Rebecca became a doctor.

World War II was the most violent and destructive conflict in history. It lasted from 1939 to 1945. By the time it was over, more than 15 million soldiers and 35 million civilians had died. Six million of these civilians were Jews who were murdered in Nazi death camps. Murdered because a little man with a Charlie Chaplin mustache considered them to be inferior. How many Nobel Prize winners were lost? The world will never know.

Novels by Anne Schraff

PASSAGES
An Alien Spring
Bridge to the Moon (Sequel to *Maitland's Kid*)
The Darkest Secret
Don't Blame the Children
The Ghost Boy
The Haunting of Hawthorne
Maitland's Kid
Please Don't Ask Me to Love You
The Power of the Rose (Sequel to *The Haunting of Hawthorne*)
The Shadow Man
The Shining Mark (Sequel to *When a Hero Dies*)
A Song to Sing
Sparrow's Treasure
Summer of Shame (Sequel to *An Alien Spring*)
To Slay the Dragon (Sequel to *Don't Blame the Children*)
The Vandal
When a Hero Dies

PASSAGES 2000
The Boy from Planet Nowhere
Gingerbread Heart
The Hyena Laughs at Night
Just Another Name for Lonely (Sequel to *Please Don't Ask Me to Love You*)
Memories Are Forever

PASSAGES to History
Dear Mr. Kilmer
Dream Mountain
Hear That Whistle Blow
Strawberry Autumn
Winter at Wolf Crossing